Dim, Doga Robot

Sudhanshu Shekhar

ISBN 978-93-5610-325-2
© Sudhanshu Shekhar 2022
Published in India 2022 by Pencil

Contributors:
Co-Author: Sudhanshu Shekhar

A brand of
One Point Six Technologies Pvt. Ltd.
123, Building J2, Shram Seva Premises,
Wadala Truck Terminal, Wadala (E)
Mumbai 400037, Maharashtra, INDIA
E connect@thepencilapp.com
W www.thepencilapp.com

Author biography

Hello, my name is Sudhanshu Shekhar. And i am an english writer. And i live in Darbhanga, Bihar, India.

I have completed my education from Bihar itself.

CONTENTS

Preface

There was a scientist Ahiam, who invented incorrect invention. It was again shed the nature. So that was a incorrect robot. But he died then his son Dim boy invented the right robot. And got the command over his father robot.

But in the story thieves made the Dim boy a cyborg.

Ch1 Gift of his father

One flying paper aeroplane, two flying paper aeroplanes and the many flying paper aeroplanes were
flying from the window by Dim boy. They are catch by flying bug and enjoying by reading the message
and recording it. It is the story of 2080 year. Where Dim house was a flat located on 14th floor. And his
father was a scientist. The name of his father was Ahiam . He works at Lubri laboratory at India. He was
a mechanical scientist of robot. When Ahiam enters in to laboratory by soccer instead of lift of 2018
century? He was happy by joining his colleague. He has five colleagues. Working on a project of robot.
The name of the robot was Doga. And it was still in process. All his colleagues pay the attention for
working on robot. But there is always a mistake and all suppose becomes illegal. As no one going to does
the suppose which is right. As it was hard and goes high from his entire mind. Then also they were trying
to make the Doga robot.
But in making robot he has a mistake that the space agency Mac was stopping in
making robot. He has a believe that the robot of Ahiam is again shed the human and works for the bad
person. So there is restriction in making robot. But then also Ahiam was interested in making robot by

ridding him.

He always thinks of a comfort zone while making robot of a key hole in robot heart and

making a robot key. So his project was inappropriate because the robot always hits the wrong answer

while it was in making. So there was wrong key for him. Ahiam tolerated many times with his colleagues

but then also it was a mistake in making robot. Ahiam thinks that why don't he keep the words of Mac

space agency? But he thinks in positive to make the robot. He was making the robot with gravity. But he

was always failed. As robot works for another future. Looks like work for the bad company. Ahiam

always manipulate the construction chapter, robot feature, robot temperature, robot dependency,

robot version, and robot equation on maths. But he with his colleague was failed.

Aiham has a two month only last to work on robot. So from working in his laboratory he comes at his

home by flying car. His flying car was above in the air and returns at his gate. And click the car for the

upstairs garage. His car automatically flies and stops at the upstairs garage by living Ahiam.

Now Ahiam

was at his home. His son was 20 year old and about to join the college. His college was in Delhi. And he

lives at 50 km. away from the college. And from his future car it takes few hours to come at college.

Then at home he was doing his college work with the help of abacus. His father came at the gate and

there is a camera inside his home. From the camera his son Dim saw his father. Then he presses the password. And the gate opens. It was Ahiam son Dim, who opens the gate?

Now he opens the digital window as a TV. As the TV. Is not present in his age instead of that there is a

flying screen of air which also supports the message. Now it comes the news which was that if planet

war spread to earth then no one will be alive. There was the news of planet war on other planet. And

the other news about the crime of thieves of earth. And then it closes the flying screen as per suggestion

of his father. His father told him to join the dinner and Dim with his father joins the dinner at dining

table. They ate too much and then his father told that after dinner he has something special to give it

was a cube of puzzle if he solves the puzzle then he will have a master key to run any robot which has

the key power to run. So Ahiam gave the puzzle to his son Dim. Now Dim was going to watch day dream

as his choice. Then he opens the Ludo box with another key and put the father's key in a rack of his

home. Then he was watching the day dream that a magician was killing a fairy and after the power of

fairy came she kills the evil magician. His entire dream was naked with his eyes. Then his father with his

future car goes for the friend club. Where he will play the game. His father meets with his wife at his

home. She was a housewife and Ahiam told his wife to take care of Dim.

Ch2 Friends of Ahiam and his son too

Ahiam reaches at his friends club. He opens the club door with the help of poem password and a little

key was the protection. Thus Ahiam enters in to club. There were five colleagues, three man and two

women playing billiards games and talking about the U.F.O. warning. Then it came Ahiam in the mid of

the game, took the stick and began playing with ball. Now the speech between them changes. They talk

about his project on Doga robot. He changes the mind frequency of Doga robot many times but then

also it was intolerable for him. Still Doga robot works for the bad person. So there was hurdle in making

robot.

The names of his colleague were Picu, Neak, Trave, Rosy and Siyre. All of them enjoying the game.

And the other side Dim was making a maths club at his home of another room. He submitted many like

Ludo, Puzzle, Business, game and the geometry three dimension game then he made the construction

and leaved the room. Now he wants to call his friend too with the help of mobile phone, he takes the

mobile and ring to his friend. The name of his friends were Saniya, Gopu and Gorya. All of his friends

were on a single voice call. So they talk about the math

club. And also his dignity at the school. One of
his friend Gopu was a good cheater. So when Dim saw
that he is cheating a love message from his mind
then he was caught. So a difference arises in him and Dim.
Now Dim was at his home finished the all
three voice call. And was waiting for his father. His father
came at his home. And talks with him. He talks
that Dim you have to be a intelligent person as in your
college there is allowance of robot making
program. So i have few old chart papers in which there is a
making of robot techniques so all of this put
in your maths club as i heard from you about the maths
club,. And never forget to solve the puzzle of
key and get the master key for the all robot. It is your best
gift from him. When the time will come then
automatic the puzzle will open and it works for any robot?
Then his son asked on which project he is
working, his father replied that he is working for a Doga
robot in which there is a always a bad mentality
for the robot. So how the robot works for the good will
we don't know? Now Dim was satisfied with his
father.
Now it comes the call of Mac space agency to Ahiam that
please come at his centre to work on the
quantum robot which works without key. Now he was
reporting Mac space agency. Then he goes on
soccer underground. Where best scientist works with high
labour? Now it came the Ahiam and told
hello to all his friend scientist. Then Ahiam asks for the
master. The scientist told him that he is busy on
another planet. Which is other than earth? It was on mars
where he is fighting from the thieves?

Then

Ahiam began working on quantum robot. It was a real tackle of his program. He changes the program

and works for the new program. He searched the bug. And then it was a automatic work on system. The

system began working and the robot work was finished in at most three hour. Now it was time for

leave, he shacked his hand with scientist and collected own project of Doga robot. And came at his

laboratory. He put the collected project on desk and came at his home.

Ch3 News of thieves

In the 2080 century no one believes in hero. As the hero was only a subject matter. But then also there
was a need of making hero. For need of everything is always real. Also when it talks about the thieves. It
was a risky. For he has eyes on many thing. As the thieves has a dead list in which there was the name of
Lubri laboratory. And also thieves lives on other planet. some time they enter in our space by making
bad plan to does the thievery. Within any of the day the thieves if see the good plan of making any robot
then he can catch it. As this entire thing Ahiam was not knowing. Also the superior of Mac laboratory
was not known of the fact. Also it was two months time in making robot of Ahiam.
There was a gang of
thieves, name of the gang was Hemming bird. In which the main leader was Picota. And there was
another gang; name of the other gang was lizard of thieves. The name of the leader was Bopo. They
fight at another planet. And those who wins, he comes on earth from outer space for thievery. As there
was split in the thieve gang. And it was created by the master of planet who lives in Mac space agency.
So there is always fight in two gangs.

As the Ahiam knows the master of planet he has a good relationship
with master. So as a wisher Ahiam and master has a good friendship bond. As the master name was
Egoeye. And he lives at Mac agency at France.
When Ahiam returns at home he opens the digital globe in which there was a live recording of
master Egoeye. He told in his digital speech that you should work on another project instead of Doga
robot. As Doga robot is dangerous to society. If you finish the project then it will harm you. but then also
Ahiam recorded and send a message that he is all right with his project. Everything will be all right with
the invention of key robot that was Doga. He understand that it was danger then also he wants to make
the robot Doga. Then the digital call disconnected.
Then at the other next day
Ahiam joins the lecture in the college of Dim. He sometime comes in the college for lecture as a chief
guest. So that was his big lecture in the class room about the robot that robot is a machine that is
programmable by the computer and capable of caring complex actions. Robot may be designed to take
the human form and works at the function of human.....
Thus he finished his lecture.
And Ahiam came at his
home. At home he dictated everything to his son Dim that he is working on a project of dangerous
Robot that is Doga. He has made the last key and if he supply last key to Doga robot then it will began
working. If it will be properly then it will be high price for him otherwise he has to carry the loss.

Then his
father was making future aeroplane of paper and fly into air to read the message out of window by the
cyber bug. As cyber bug was everywhere to play with people. So Dim and his father Ahiam both played the game.
His father also told him that he likes him and his friend also. So why don't he keep the party at home by
flying the digital screen everywhere and joins of his friend. Now he uses his future car to go in market.
Market was full of party object; from there Ahiam buys the balloon and party song. Now he returns at his home.
At his home Dim was busy in playing turtle game so he asked his father Ahiam that what is the
story of turtle game. His father answered his entire question that there is a son turtle who protects his home from the monster cockroach?
Now his father told the Dim that please call his friend for party at his
home. All the arrangement has been done. The digital flying screen was travelling everywhere. And thus
then hello. It comes the guests. The dance show and speech of his dear home. All was inviting the
happiness. His father has called five colleagues and his son has called his friends too. The Dim has a girl
friend in the party his girl friend name was Saniya. So Dim talks his girl friend that how much she loves
him. She also told that she loves him too much. Dim mother also enjoying the party. Party makeup was
right. Then there is end of the party. All dismissed at there home it was too night. They arrange the

future car and return their home.

Then at next day there is observation of robot Doga by the Ahiam and his colleagues.

He saw a key in Doga robot's heart which was link by the someone. So he saw the scene in camera. He

found that three thieves came inside his Lubri laboratory. And tries to harm the robot but he was unable

as the robot behaviour was abnormal and not fine. As the robot automatic tries to work for the evil. So

Ahiam was working to correct the robot. But he was unable. So it was his last two chance. Thus he came

at his home.

Ch4 Doga robot runs from laboratory

Ahiam son Dim has his girlfriend Saniya. Who was at her home? So Dim came at the Saniya home and he saw that the doors were open. He enters in to door. He saw that Saniya was taking bath. So he saw first time to any lady to take bath open. He saw from a glass. Then two detective butterfly who were flying outside the room saw the Dim. So the two butterflies complained the matter to Saniya. Then Saniya told Dim to wait in the another room. Dim told her that you are looking beautiful. Then also Saniya requested him to wait in another room. Then Saniya shuts the room and Dim goes to another room for waiting Saniya.

After bath Saniya was dressed in a colourful dress and then talks with Dim. Dim told her that he has come at his home to collect his first robot project of college as per his father had taught.

Saniya helps him in this work then Saniya told the Dim to take coffee. So he told his home robot to make coffee. As Saniya was rich then Dim so he called the robot and given him the coffee. The coffee was hard and then after some time he returns at his home.

At home Dim talks to his father as father has called him to talk. He talks about his robot project. He talks that

never believe in evilness it always lie infront of
every sphere but you don't have to believe. So Dim asked
to his father that why he is talking like this.
Then father wants to reply about his Doga robot that he is
another kind of robot but his work function is
evil. Only he has to correct it. But he didn't told anything
about the robot or his evilness. His father
thinks that he is his project. So he should work.
Then next day Dim was about to visit his college. He was
on
the future car. So he lands at his college by flying down. As
the future car flies in to air. Then Dim meets
with his friend Saniya . Dim wants to propose her. But he
was cool. So when Saniya came infront of him
Dim proposed him. Saniya accepted his propose. So both
are in love.
Then Dim came at his home. At his
home his mother told him that his father is no more in this
world. Dim asked what happened to his
father. His mother told that as your father was a robot
scientist. So in his laboratory Lubri he was
working on a dangerous robot. The name of the robot was
Doga he was a evil robot. As your father
wants to correct the robot. But he was unable. As his last
key trapped in the heart key hole and the
robot kills your father and ran away. As the experiment
failed.
So all this news was not accepted by Dim so he visited
his Lubri laboratory in the lab he saw the camera. And he
saw how his five colleagues left alive but his
father died. Because of Doga robot. So in laboratory it
comes a call of Egoeye master he told that he is

sorry about his father. Then he told about the another project of robot. For he was selected by Mac

space agency. He told that he always stops the Ahiam to make the robot but it was not so. Your father

has constructive mind but then also he was working on a dangerous project. Also the talk of master

doesn't ignore by any one. But your father ignores my talk. So you don't work on dangerous project. And

must be positive project.

Ch5 Doga meets with thief

The seven days passed. There was no news of any robot like Doga. The all society of Dim including him
has got the fear about robot. So Dim called the police to catch the robot.
The robot Doga when ran from
Lubri laboratory he came at vegetable place of the market. There the robot was correcting him in
illusion. There he searches the thieves. Noticing the Doga robot. Then robot told own opportunity to
thieves after meeting him. He was right he ask two thieves. That he is his friend not friend of the good
person. He will works for him. And he is made for evil human. The two thieves want to take the test.
Then he given doga a heavy machine gun by taking him the alone side of vegetable market. So now Doga
robot thinks that he has a good mechanism for work. And he is free from idiot scientist. So Doga told to
his friend thieves that what he should do? The friend told him that only you keep eyes on attacking
person otherwise he will attack. As i have the strong power. Actually you don't have to fight. So two
thieves called the other thieves to meet him the best robot of city. As no one kill him if he uses own
strong power. The all thieves after meeting become happy.

Then it came the news of master in the digital
globe of Dim. The master told him still you are sad. Master
Egoeye still has the deep sympathy with you
and with your father who died. Then Dim told to master
Egoeye that my father told me that never give
up in the any war have faith on us. So his last words were
this. Then master Egoeye told him that you
have anything left with your father precious object. Dim
told yes. He has a puzzle master key. How i can
solve it i don't know. But my father told me that after me
you can solve the puzzle. Then master Egoeye
told him to bring the puzzle. Then Dim brought the
puzzle. It was a cube rotating in three *four bricks. It
was in my both hand. Then i began to rotate but before
my beginning it has become small and a key
came out of it. It was a master key. Dim was happy to see
that
But master Egoeye wants to take the
master key as he needs. So Dim gave the master key to
master Egoeye. Then master told Dim that you
have a project on the Doga 2 robot. As your father died in
making Doga 1robot project. As that was a
bad project and you have to work on good project of
Doga 2. When the Doga 2 project will be finish he
will give the master key to finish the project of Dim. Also
it's a opportunity for you to take the revenge
from Doga 1 robot.

Ch6 Dim was interested in making project

Dim family was in depression. His mother was sad from long time. Also Dim girlfriend was giving
sympathy to his mother. And Dim too was silent and sad. As his father was no more.
But then also Dim
asked his mother that there is a project of making robot Doga 2. His mother first avoided but at second
she asked the detail of project. Then Dim has given the details of project. It was a secure project given
by Mac space agency. Thus Dim will work.
As Dim knows many things from his father. His father had told
Dim many things about the robot. So Dim was interested in making project of Doga 2.

Ch 7 The thieves and Doga 1

When Doga 1 robot was found then all the thieves meet at a place. At a place they did the meeting. That what they should do to Doga 1 robot? As it was strong robot. So at first they need money so they make a plan to loot the bank with the help of Doga 1 robot. They came at the Munchi bank at Delhi. And they does the rob as in the hand of robot Doga was a heavy machine gun. He was at the door of Munchi bank. So the thieves does the robbery and ran away. Then media came. And distributed the news of robot and thieves on the air digital channel. As everything was captured in the eye. So Dim was watching the news. When he saw the robot Doga 1 he became angry. As his father died because of Doga 1 robot. So he wants to take the revenge. But how he doesn't know. Then master Egoeye came in the digital window and asked the Dim that, you have to close the Lubri laboratory. And work with us at Mac space laboratory with the specialist. Here you can make strong robot than Doga 1. For i have concluded by your master key. Your master key will work to make strong robot. The robot must be stronger than Doga 1 robot. And then we will take revenge of your father with Doga 1 robot. Then the digital window closed.

Then next day Dim was

visiting college and in the college at lunch time he saw that there is attack of Doga 1 robot. As the Doga

1 robot with the thieves had meeting arranged that he will kill the human who defeat him? As the news

of Egoeye master was secretly spread to thieves with the help of another bug. So there is attack on

college. The Dim when saw the attack; he ran from the college with the help of future car and came at

his home. He then calls the master Egoeye. Master Egoeye fixes the two body guard robot at his door of

home. And he spreads detective bug in all direction of his home. Then they were at home. After

sometime master Egoeye came at Dim home. Dim respected him. Egoeye master told the Dim that there

is spread of his news to the thieves. Thieves also know the news with the help of detective bug. so there

is small problem. Then Dim was in problem he told how he can do the class. If there is attack. Egoeye

master also told that you are right as Doga 1 robot is strong. And also he is searching you in his memory.

And there is another news of planet war which will spread to the earth by the thieves. So there is need

of making Doga 2 robot. Thus master Egoeye called the Dim on the other part of the earth where the

Mac space agency was located.

So there were present of many robots, alien and quantum computers

with arms. There Dim meets with the five colleague of his father also there he meets with a young lady

name Shripa who has permission to keep robot? All robot

works on the falling of quantum computer.

And Shripa was the owner of many robots. Thus she gave the permission to his specialist and his

colleagues to work on the Doga 2 robot. Which will work on master key? As Dim's father has made the

key.

Then there is attack on earth with Doga 1 robot. All where was the loot and kill of many human? The

earth of India was full of inhuman. So police of earth without master Egoeye cannot do anything. Thus

police of earth was active but then also they were defeated by the thieves as Doga 1 robot does the

difficult task in the fight. So police was unable to win the war.

Ch8 Dim with his girlfriend

When Dim was chosen the scientist of Mac space agency
his girl friend feels happy. And told to him that
you must take the revenge of your father. As Doga 1 is a
dangerous robot. Then she gave a love letter:-
In the love letter:-
Dear Dim,
You don't know how much i love you? As you are my be
love and i am your be love. You love me and i
love you. Everything will be all right when you will take the
action again shed Doga 1 robot. And it will be
near so please take care of you.
Your be lover:-
Saniya
Dim mother too wishes. Now Dim came at Mac space
agency. There he meets with colleagues and
specialist and at last before the beginning of work Dim has
to take the permission from Shripa. The head
of the Mac agency.
Then it began
the work. There was a Skelton of robot and then the
wiring from the computer. And then a key is added.
The key was like a zig zag so it did not work. The making
of Doga 2 robot was different. Now there is
leave plan of Dim, for working the next day.

So next day still there was a making of heart of Doga 2 robot. It
uses many keys but how it gets the stronger Dim doesn't know. So he has to make it carefully. He added
many wire in a nuclei of heart but it sparks all time and it does not work. Then it again try for next day.
At the next day it came news that out of five agent one agent the name Neak died. It was the work of
Doga 1robot. He killed the Neak and left a letter that anyone who is interested in making robot Doga 2.
He will be the target of him.
So Shripa and master Egoeye gets a deep regret for this. And Dim too gets
feared.
Now master Egoeye and police want to search the Doga 1 robot. And they had a hard detective and
protection around him. Then Dim will make the Doga 2 robot.
It was 7th days passed, Dim was still continuous
in making Doga 2 project then he will defeat Doga 1 robot. Now at the end of 20th days Doga 2
continuous in making and it got completed.
Now it needs a practise for fighting with one robot with other
robot. From this stamina and strategy, he will decide to fight with other robot.

Ch9 Competition first

In the first competition Doga 2 robot has to fight with the
computer robot of Mrs. Shirpa. So Dim was
teaching the fight scene to Doga 2. Doga 2 always in his
memory a little fight scene. Always he was fail to
fight. Dim always added the new memory and new key to
Doga 2 robot. But all was fail. Then also the
time reaches for fight in a ring it was rope from all side and
Doga 2 has to fight from computer robot.
Then
master Egoeye came and told me the hello. And also told
how the preparation is? I told the preparation
is well. Let's see in the ring. I was giving the answer but
that was not correct answer. I also told "the
technique of my robot is fine." But in my opinion," The
Doga 2 need more practise. I teach him many
lesson of fight. But then also the memory of Doga 2 robot
was short. I ask the Doga 2 that would you
fight right. As without practise you cannot fight with the
Doga 1 robot as it need more practise and also
you are made for the fight of Doga 1 robot." The master
Egoeye was very much ready for the fight.
The fight begins the computer robot hit the Doga 2 robot.
The Doga 2 robot had got a hard punch from
computer robot. The robot falls down on earth. And it had

a great complication. But then also all was
right. All the programmer of Mac agency was watching the
fight of Doga 2. Again Doga 2 stands from
ground but this time also he was fail. There was no
atmosphere of winning Doga 2 robot. But then also
he fights. Then his neck was broken with another punch
and it stops the fight. The shripa was happy to
see that the Doga 2 robot was not working the good than
other robot. For she already shake hands with
thieves and she was a conspirator in Mac space agency. No
one knows even the master Egoeye.
So at the end of fight the Doga 2 robot again was made for
the experiment. The key hole was locked
and it joints the neck. And he was lived alone to does the
experiment. He was practising in a punch bag
of iron and that was his best afford from his side. I ask the
robot that how he is at fighting. The robot
told don't worry we will win the fight. Then Dim was
thinking how he could make smart robot. For this
he does hard labour. Then it comes the master Egoeye.
Master also helps in making robot. He told that if
the master key he will use then no one has the power to
win Doga 2 robot. Now he is busy. After
winning the competition he will add the master key for
fighting with Doga 1 and thieves. Then he went
from there.

Ch10 Competition two

The next day Doga 2 was keen observation by the specialist. The specialist again made the Doga 2 robot
for fight. Again in the ring Doga 2 robot step down. And it began the fight. The Doga 2 gave a hard punch
to Shirpa robot. And one robot break down and falls on earth. Then the bell rang. It comes the next
robot for fighting. The next robot was good in fighting so he gave a hard punch in Doga 2 heart the key
broke and Doga 2 began telling absurd. The game was over. Again Shripa feels happy. The game was
over. Now specialist catches the Doga 2 robot and went for laboratory. All the labour of Dim was looking
absurd now.
It was a digital call of thieves in the house of Shripa. She talks with thieves that Doga 2has
not won any fight. And it was a good news for that. If he will win the fight then he will give the copy of
Doga 2. Use it in Doga 1. Then the digital call disconnected.
Now the specialist along with colleague was
following the procedure in making Doga 2 robot. They were doing hard labour. Now they were feeling
the procedure that all was good in making. Then the commands were entered in to Doga 2 robot. Doga

2 robot replied the command. Doga 2 told in his robotic tone that welcome please enter the command.

Then his owner Dim entered the many commands the robot swing his hand and all was a starting. Then

Dim entered key inside the key hole inside the heart and it began working. Doga 2 showing some special

effect on effect run. Doga 2 was ready for the third competition.

Now it came a letter from Dim's

girlfriend. In the letter it was written that :-

Dear Dim,

Everything is right. But i am remembering you from my depth of heart. It went long time while going

Mac space agency. Reply the true matter. What is the invention of Doga 2?

There is only one problem in

the city that everywhere the thieves walk. They kill any of the innocent and loot also. This was a

scoundrel news which is coming in our news daily.

Your lovely:-

Saniya

Then Dim listened the letter which was sent in a bug inside a computer system. Then Dim replied

another letter in same bug as bug was a different media of talking. Then in the other letter it was replied

that.

Dear Saniya,

If you listen and watch me inside the computer system. Then listen me i have meant two competition of

Doga 2. But it was useless. Then also i make preparation to work for the correctness of Doga 2. And it

works also so within a month i will be completing project.

Then we shall marry. What about my mother.

She was not seen in the computer monitor system. Then Dim told fine, i will meet her later.

Your boyfriend:-

Dim

Then within another second Dim's mother was calling. She sent blessing to Dim and works with secure.

Take the experiment on robot carefully and you to be careful. I heard much news about Doga 1 as he

has got the destructive mind and created a bad mind impression on us by loot with thieves. They have

collected too much money from the planet bank and now they were in order to does the experiment on

another planet. As your master Egoeye told us. So be careful about yourself.

Then in another talk a digital window connected to him and Dim was connected to his mother digital

computer system. He was talking right. And told that the project will finish within a month. And he will

be at home. As he wants to marry with Saniya. As told earlier.

Ch 11 Competition third

Doga 2 was preparing for the next fight as an examine then it looks well with the fight between the Doga
1 robot. As it is matter of Dim's father impression. Doga 2 was real. And his invention was real. Only he
need a master key. Which master Egoeye can offer? Then also without the master key Doga 2 was
retuning with his memory. He has a different type of memory other than Doga 1. Doga 1 robot after,
great thinking it comes the weakness in him the key which my father was invented was not good. But he
has given the best master key to me. So he was great. Now Shripa loaded the two computer with full of
memory to fight with Doga 2 robot. Doga2 robot told he can fight with two robot. Then Dim was ready
two press the key hole in his heart. The robot was all right in the ring. But one computer robot came and
gave a punch to Doga 2 but Doga 2 fights for that he easily defeated two robots. Shirpa became upset
she thinks that definitely Doga 1 will lose the fight. Otherwise he has to kill the Doga 2 robot. Then Doga
2 robot keep his mouth shut as server was shut and called other robot who was stronger then him. At
first he loses the fight but at another second he wins the war.

Now the fight ends Dim saw the robot and shake his hands

with him and told today you have got positive result. Doga 2 also said i like you. Then Dim told please

wait at the canteen, i am coming from meeting with master Egoeye. As Shripa was behind the robot. So

he came at Doga 2 robot. The robot told what can i do for you? The shirpa told i am your friend side that

is Dim. He told me that please shut down your system. Then Doga 2 shut down his system. And shripa

now collected the data and given to thieves. And someone watching the Shripa from behind. He was

Trave one of his colleague. He search the Shripa that he is contacting two thieves by digital globe of two

gang. Also there was a news that there will be meeting of thieves. So be alert. Now Doga 2 was weaker

than Doga 1. Trave was hiding and watching all this.

And the other side Dim goes to meet the master Egoeye and master

Egoeye told that there is meeting of the gangs of the thief and i am sure that he is experimenting on

someone at the other side of the planet.

Then Trave came in hurry before the master Egoeye. And told

everythinh about the conspiracy of Shripa. Then dim was missing the robot so he came at canteen. He

saw that the robot is shut down and also his data is loot. So he pays an attention. And called master

Egoeye to call Shripa. Shripa at first was liar. But after sometime she told what you can do? As our

power is bigger than you. we are planet thieves and soon

we will fight with you. Then master Egoeye
arrested the Shripa and sent in planet prison.

Ch 12 Competition four

As Shripa arrested then Dim's colleagues arranged the fight for practise and examing. The fight was
tough then also other memory of Doga 2 wins the fight. And told to Dim that he is ready for fight with
Doga 1. As Doga 2 was our genius invention. Then master told i have a wish of your father. First we will
check the gravity and then the current in wire and without spark the right neuron in mind and the
matching key all was waste only master key was perfect so master Egoeye added master key in the heart
of Doga 2. Then the outcome was sparkling. The robot work function stops for a moment. And then it
works fast as faster than the computer bits of computer. All was right invention.

Ch 13 True friends

As Dim has completed his project with new invention. So
he wants to walk with his girlfriend to another
planet with the permission from his master Egoeye. Master
Egoeye gave the permission. Dim was
allowed to walk in spaceship. Then they roam to mars.
Where he meets with an alien character Bruno. It
was a hot planet and alien live to stay there he was in fairy
market of alien. Where every technology sold
with the cheap price. Dim too buys few techniques with
the help of Bruno. Bruno helps the Dim in every
step. And Bruno has the information of every planet. As
he has few meter in his height. And when he ask
about the Doga 1? He was amazing. So he keeps fight with
Doga 1. Then Dim buys some kind of
weapon. The techniques were some kind of drone. Then
they return at earth. And at the earth he made
friendship with Bruno by giving him a mouth organ as a
gift. And Bruno also came on earth.
When Dim and his
girl friend along with Bruno came on earth. There was a
meeting in Mac space agency with master and
other planet people. They have told that there are five base
of thieves in which they were doing wrong
experiment. So we have to stop them. Four is on earth and
one at the another planet so we have to do

the planet war again shed the all thieves. Who has got
courage from the Doga 1 robot?
Now Doga 2 is ready
with master key in his heart for the planet war.
Now it was the meeting of two gang of thieves. Which
were Hemming gang the leader was Picota and other gang
was Lizard gang whose leader was Bopo.?
So they told to each other that with the coming of Doga 1
we have got the new power. Then Bopo told
that there is invention of Doga 2 so we will lose. Also Mrs.
Shripa is in prision so how we can know the
right situation of Doga 2. Then Picota told don't worry if
we fight then win also.

Ch 14 Attack on bases

It was first base. All the preparation to destroy the base has been done by the master Egoeye. Doga 2

robot was also preparing with his arms to fight with Doga 1 robot. Then at the base there was a severe

attack by the Doga 2robot but at first Doga 1robot does not have any realization. So it does not matter

with that. Now the second attack by Doga 2robot has been done then Doga 1 robot realizes that Doga 2

is power ful then master Egoeye attacks on thieves bases all were the experiment object and one by one

master Egoeye destroyed the experiment object. The thief when saw that he his defeating then he ran

from there. some caught and some success in running. Also Doga 1 does not fight and ran from there.

Now it was the

second base all the preparation had done the thieves to fight again shed the MACspace agency and

police. For it was the second fight. And they known that there must be attack. All were in plan that this

time he will not leave master Egoeye and Doga 2. So this was the tough war between master Egoeye ,

Doga 2 ,thieves and Doga 1. Doga 2 has attack hard to Daoga 1 earlier. But this time they are with map

of experiment base. So secretly they entered into

laboratory. And killed the two thieves on the gate. As
it was the plan of master Egoeye. And work done by the
Doga 2 robot. Then they move forward at
forward there was a protection of Doga 1 robot. So Doga
2 robot fights with Doga 1 robot. At first they
fight with arms. But in a few second they come closer and
attacks both by hand Dim was also there he
told don't leave this Doga 1 robot. As he is the killer of my
father. So Doga 2 attacks fast. As Doga 2 was
winning the fight with hand. Then it comes the head of the
gang Bopo thief. He supplied gun to Doga
1robot and Doga 2 robot also got the gun from master
Egoeye. So fight between Doga 2 robot and Doga
1 robot was long time. Now master Egoeye enters into
next level of base it was third base closed with
each other and bombarded on it with the help of bomb.
All the thieves died.
Now at base four on earth Dim has also arrow and bow to
fight
again shed the thieves. He has the modern arms. When
thief knows that there is attack on base four
they comes at the helipad on roof of the building and told
Doga 1 robot to fight and stop them down the
roof. So Doga 1 robot was fighting with all of the team of
police then Doga 2 robot came forward and
protected the police and fights with Doga 1 robot. Doga 2
robot told the Dim boy to come forward and
go upstairs and fight with the thieves as they are running
from base to other planet. so Dim came
forward but then also thieves kidnapped Dim as his
weapon was finish so thieves kidnapped Dim boy.
Then thieves along with Dim boy flies from there. To

another planet by changing helicopter in to space
ship. The thieves came at other planet. Which was
supposed planet where he was doing experiment?
Also the Doga 1 robot had been arrested by the police
with the help of Doga 2 robot. And he has been
shut down by removing key from his heart.

Ch 15 Blackmail

Now it arises a dispute between thieves, police and Mac space agency for returning Dim boy. There was
a threaten to Mac space agency that if he will not return Doga 1 robot then he might make the Dim boy
a cyborg. The Mac space agency wants the planet war to kill all thieves who is living on another planet .
So Mac space agency was taking the help of another planet by sending cyber bug to all those planet who
can help.
So all planet people collected at a place with space ship and master Egoeye told to all friends we
should not live all the thieves of another planet we must attack on him. So there was a big attack from
master Egoeye side. But before the attack Dim boy was taken into experiment and he has been
converted in to cyborg. So when Doga 2 watch this while visiting at Dim boy. The Dim boy was the slave
of thieves and fighting again shed the right people. So Doga 2 saw a coding at his brain if that coding will
be destroyed then he might be converted in to our people. So only this hope was left. There was fight
between thieves and police, aliens Mac space agency and master Egoeye.
So after a big attack all of them killed

the thieves. Also the two gang thieves head has been killed including gang too broke. And Dim was
release after a big effort of Doga 2 robot and master Egoeye. Now he is not left his brain coding has
been removed after a big effort. And the war was over.

Ch 16 Planet earth

On after returning to planet earth Dim was not liked by his
mother only his girlfriend and master Egoeye
and Bruno likes him. For Dim boy is now cyborg.

www.ingramcontent.com/pod-product-compliance
Lightning Source LLC
LaVergne TN
LVHW050426160726
843469LV00041B/1252